SANDA

The Girl with the Magical Smile

ISBN 13: 978-1-63489-146-2

Library of Congress Catalog Number: 2018957233
Printed in the United States of America
First Printing: 2018
22   21   20   19   18   5   4   3   2   1

Cover and interior design by Aurora Whittet.

Wise Ink Creative Publishing
807 Broadway St. NE, Suite 46
Minneapolis, MN 55413
wiseink.com

To order, visit itascabooks.com or call 1-800-901-3480. Reseller discounts available.

This book is for you, Dad—thank you for loving me.
— Sabina

*To my aunt Sabby, thank you for giving me the opportunity
to use my skills for this book.*
— Ntuli

Sanda

The Girl with the Magical Smile

Sabina Mugassa Bingman

ILLUSTRATED BY Ntuli Aswile

Once upon a time in Tanzania, over a century ago, there lived a girl who loved to smile. Her name was Sanda. No matter how hard things were, Sanda shared her beautiful smile and kindness with others.

Sanda lived in small village on Ukerewe, the biggest island in Lake Victoria. Sanda had lost her parents at young age, and now she lived with her aunt Nandele and her cousin Mune. Sanda and Mune did everything together: swimming, dancing, playing games, and even chores. Mune was her best friend.

"Muneeee....," Sanda called one day from her place under the mango tree in front of their straw-roofed home. "Mune, njoo tafadhali—Please come here."

Mune responded from one of the two bedrooms, "Nakuja! Subiri kidogo—Wait a minute, I am coming!" A moment later she came outside. "What do you need, Sanda?" Mune asked, a sparkle in her eyes.

"I am heading to the lake. Would you like to come with me?" Sanda said, smiling.

"Sawa—Okay! We can go swimming!" Mune replied.

"Yes, we can! I need to wash my clothes too," said Sanda.

"Aw, can't you do that another time?" Mune said.

"Nope, that would be a bad idea," Sanda said.

"Why?" Mune asked.

"Because all my clothes are dirty! Besides, you may need to wash yours too!"

"Ohhh, fine, I can get mine too," Mune said. She did, and the two took off running to the lake.

Everyone in the village liked Sanda, who was loving and respectful to everyone. She helped her elderly neighbors when they needed to fetch water or gather sticks for making a fire. She helped younger kids to find food and taught them their letters or numbers. She was always ready to lend a hand where it was needed.

That day, as she headed home from the lake with her clean clothes, she saw Mzee Sulusi struggling to get all his chickens in the coop, where they would be safe overnight. *(Mzee means "old man" in Kiswahili; it is a very respectful way of speaking to one's elders.)*

"Shikamoo, Mzee Sulusi," Sanda greeted her neighbor. She giggled a little because it was funny to see Mzee Sulusi running back and forth as the chickens darted out of the coop and between his legs.

"Marahaba, Sanda! Hujambo?—How are you doing?" Mzee Sulusi responded.

"Sijambo—I am well," Sanda said. "You look like you could use some help. I can get the chickens in, Mzee Sulusi."

"Oh, ahsante—Thank you, Sanda," he said. "That would be great. These chickens are so clever! At my age I can't keep up with them."

Sanda got to work. "Shuhhh shhh, kuku ...sheishhh.....sheishhh! Kuku, there you go...." In no time she had chased all the chickens into their coop.

"Problem solved: they are all in!" Sanda said with her big grin.

"I knew you could do better job than this here mzee!" He chuckled. "Thank you, Sanda! Wewe ni mtoto mzuri—You are a good kid!"

Sanda smiled and clasped her hands. "Usihofu—Don't worry!" she told him. "Next time just leave this job to me."

"Hurry home now," Mzee Sulusi said. "It is getting late, and your aunt will be looking for you."

"Haya. Usiku mwema! Kwaheri!" Sanda responded—"Okay. Good night! Goodbye!"

"Ahsante, kwaheri," Mzee Sulusi replied—"Thank you! Goodbye!"

Sanda was a very joyful girl, good-hearted and generous like her parents, and everyone in the village loved her. Everyone, that is, but Aunt Nandele, who was jealous of her niece and treated her very harshly. But no one knew how difficult Sanda's life was except Mune.

That evening, Sanda tripped while getting a cup of water for her aunt. "Ouch!" she exclaimed. "Oh no, my ankle. Mmmh."

"You stupid girl!" Aunt Nandele yelled.

"Samahani, Aunt—I am sorry! It was an accident," Sanda said with a fearful look.

"Toka! Toka hapa!—Go, go away!" her aunt yelled.

Sanda went outside and sat down on the big curved rock under the mango tree. She was unhappy, but she did not stay sad for long. She started thinking of the exciting day that was coming soon. The people of Sanda's village had a very old tradition of carving their top front teeth to sharp points when they about thirteen years old. When a girl got her teeth carved, people spoke well of her. The process was painful, and the girls who did it were certainly brave, strong, and responsible, as well as beautiful. The tradition had been passed down for generations.

Sanda and her friends had been looking forward to getting their teeth carved for a long time. There was one special lady who was known for doing the carving well: her name was Buzina. People traveled long distances to see her, and girls wanted no one but Buzina to carve their teeth. She came to the village only twice a year, and it was nearly time for her to arrive.

Sanda and the other village girls had been preparing for months, making their teeth white and strong by brushing them and chewing sugar cane regularly. Sanda had waited for this all her life, for her mother had promised, before she passed, to take Sanda have her teeth carved.

The next day, Sanda told her friends, "Nasubiri kwa hamu kuchonga meno yangu!—I cannot wait to carve my teeth!" Then she felt sad. "I wish my parents could be here to see me," she said. "I miss them so much."

"You will be okay. Just know that you have us," said Namisana, one of the girls. "Tunakupenda—We love you!"

The other girls, Mune, Musingo, and Mtundu, all chimed in together, "Tunakupenda!"

"I love you too," Sanda said.

As the carving day neared, the village hosted many festivities: dances, music, competitions, and ululations at every corner to celebrate all the young girls who were getting their teeth done.

"Is everyone ready? I am ready!" Sanda said as the girls gathered near the lake for the swimming competition. Usually they were a noisy bunch, singing, telling stories, joking, and laughing together. But today they were all a bit nervous.

"How long does the carving take?" Mune asked curiously.

"I don't know. I was wondering about that too," Namisana said.

"Me too," said Musingo, who was usually quiet. "I am a little nervous because I heard it will be painful. The carver will use a sharp knife and a file to do the carving." She looked at all of them with wide eyes.

"Well, I heard it can take a whole day!" Mune said.

"What? Siku nzima?—A whole day? No way!" Sanda exclaimed, with disbelief on her face. "The carving is only done to the upper front teeth, so it shouldn't take a whole day!"

"Calm down!" Mune said. "I'm sure it's only a few seconds and you are done!"

"I don't think that's possible either, Mune," Sanda said.

Mune started giggling. "I was just joking," she confessed. "I just wanted to put everyone at ease."

Sanda thought for a moment. "I remember....my father told me that it can take up to twenty minutes, but not a whole day!" The other girls sighed with relief.

"Well, I just want to go and get it done, so everyone can see how more beautiful we are, how strong and responsible we are," Mtundu said.

"It will be exciting for everyone," Sanda agreed.

Then four neighbor boys showed up at the shore. They had just finished fishing for the day, and they set down their nyavu—fishing nets—and buckets filled with fresh fish, ready to relax or swim. One of them started teasing the girls, calling, "Look at you! I cannot believe you're just standing there, talking, while it is so hot and sweaty here! Are you afraid to swim? Maybe you don't know how to swim!" He let out an annoying laugh.

"Yeah, they're all wimps," teased another boy.

"No way!" shouted Mune. "Are you joking? We're better swimmers than you any day! Do you dare to race against us to the other shore?"

"Sure!" they shouted. The boys stepped into the lake, ready for challenge.

Malima, one of the boys, volunteered to be a coach and said, "Ready? Start on the count of five... Moja, mbili, tatu, nne, tano, Go!"

They all swam as fast as they could. The boys, with their long arms and strong bodies, stormed out ahead of the girls at first. But Sanda swam as hard as she could, and she passed one boy after another. In no time she was ahead, and no one could catch her.

She reached the shore first and jumped out of the water to cheer for her friends "Swim faster!" she shouted. "Come on, you can do it!" The other girls raced well, but two of the boys caught up to them at the last minute. In the end, it was a tie. The kids all laughed and slapped each other on the back as they dried off and gathered their clothes. Then the boys picked up their buckets and nets, and the girls filled their buckets with water, and they all headed home.

As they walked, Mtundu asked, "Sanda, do you have a dress picked out for your teeth carving? I bet it will be a very colorful one!"

"How did you know I have a dress already?" Sanda asked. "You are right! It is very pretty and colorful, too."

"I knew it! Everyone knows you like bright colors" Mtundu replied with a smile.

"Ni nzuri, sana—It is very beautiful," Sanda said. "My grandmother made it for my mother's tooth carving day. It is made of special cloth, and it took my grandmother four weeks to attach the beads. There are yellow, red, orange, white, and purple beads…. Well, you have to see it for yourself!" She smiled her big, beautiful smile just thinking about it.

"My mother kept the dress carefully, so I could wear it on my teeth carving day. And someday I hope I will pass it down to my own daughter," Sanda explained.

"That is amazing! I am sure it is very special to you," Mune said.

"I can't imagine how happy my mom would have been to see me in it! I miss her," Sanda said, sadness dimming her smile.

Mune assured her, "Your mom would have been so proud of you!"

Sanda's smile brightened again. "Hey, enough about me now," she said. "I would like to know what you all are going to wear."

"Mine is orange, with a lot of ruffles on the sleeves and at the bottom of the skirt," said Musingo shyly. "I tried it on this morning, and it fits perfectly!"

The other girls described their outfits too, excited for the carving day to come.

Sadly, as the long-awaited day neared, it became clear that Sanda's aunt didn't want her to go. "Why not?" Sanda asked Nandele. After all, every other girl Sanda's age was following this celebrated tradition. But Nandele didn't explain.

Sanda remembered what her mother had told her: "When that time comes, Sanda, your teeth will be beautifully done, sharp and as white as snow, and your smile will be even more beautiful!" She felt very sad. She decided she would keep asking, and she would not share her problem with anyone else. The week before the carver arrived, Sanda tried again. "Aunt Nandele...," Sanda asked.

"Yes," her aunt replied.

"Can you please let me go get my teeth done?"

"I said no!" Aunt Nandele shouted. "Don't you understand?"

"I've been good, and I do all my chores! Tafadhali...!" Sanda tried again. But Aunt Nandele still wouldn't listen.

Feeling sad and alone, Sanda walked to the mango tree near their home and threw some rocks at the fruit, hoping that a sweet, juicy treat would help her forget what had just happened. "Why would my aunt do something so mean?" she wondered.

She was so sad that she didn't hear Mune and the other girls walk up. "What's the matter? Is something wrong? You look so sad!" Mune said. Sanda told the girls what had happened, and tears started rolling down her cheeks.

"I don't know what to do," she said.

The girls hugged Sanda and tried to console her. They couldn't believe that Sanda might not be joining them for the teeth carving.

Mune soothingly said, "It's okay, I will try to talk to my mom."

"We will too!" said the other girls in one voice.

"We can go there right now and talk to her," suggested Namisana. "Maybe she will feel bad and say it was just a joke."

The girls walked Sanda back to her home and approached Nandele, who was sitting inside, knitting and humming.

"Shikamoo," the girls greeted Sanda's aunt respectfully.

"Marahaba," she replied without taking her eyes off her knitting.

Namisana asked, politely, "Please let Sanda join us for the teeth carving. We have been looking forward to it for a long time, and it is very important that we all do it together."

"You girls have no respect! It is my decision, and that's it!" Nandele yelled. "You can all go now."

"But...but...! Mom, please! Let Sanda go!" Mune begged her mother, but with no luck. None of them could help Sanda.

On the morning of the event, the girls came to see Sanda and get Mune. The girls were more beautiful than they had ever looked before. Their hair was neatly braided, and they wore sandals made of leather by a local shoemaker. They all looked lovely in their special outfits.

"Eeeh! Mmependeza sana—Wow! You all look beautiful!" Sanda said to them.

"Ooh, ahsante," replied Mtundu, Musingo, Namisana, and Mune.

"Sanda, we wish you could come with us!" Musingo added.

"We are so sad that you can't be part of this great experience. Our village has celebrated and honored it for so many years!" said Namisana.

"I wish some miracle would happen for you," Mune told her.

Sanda couldn't hide her tears at being left behind. Still, she smiled and said, "Go on, and be brave! You will all be so beautiful afterward! I am so happy for all of you!"

"Thank you, Sanda," they said.

"Good luck!" she said, and then she embraced Mune.

"You are so kind, Sanda," Mune said as she wiped her cousin's tears away. Then the girls waved to her, and off they went.

When Mune and the other girls came back to show off their teeth, everyone was in awe of how beautiful they looked. The village had prepared a feast meal of sweet potatoes, roast goat, vegetables, fresh fruits like papaya, pineapples, and mangoes, and a stiff porridge called ugali, which is made of cassava flour, with grilled and broiled fish. They drank tea, milk, orange juice, and squeezed sugarcane juice. All day and into the night, the village congratulated the girls with dances, singing, games, food, and all kinds of celebrations.

That night Sanda went to bed feeling hopeless. She would never get her teeth carved like her mother had promised. She cried herself to sleep. In the middle of the night, she had a dream. Someone was filing and carving her teeth, and then something magical happened. She abruptly woke up... but it was just a dream. Sadly, she went back to sleep.

Very early the next morning, Sanda woke at the first caw from a crow. No one else was awake. She quietly crept to her cousin's side.

"Mune!" she whispered. "Mune! Amka!—Wake up!" she said.

"What is it? It is too early," Mune said in a sleepy voice.

"I know it is early, but I need you!"

"Ohh, Sanda, I am too tired and very sleepy. Give me one more minute of sleep and I will be fine," Mune said, and she rolled over again.

Sanda replied, "Don't be silly! One minute would not change anything." But Mune said nothing. Sanda waited for a minute, and then she shook her cousin's arm and tried to pull her out of the bed.

"Please! Wake up now—it is important!" Sanda reassured her, "You will be okay after you get out of bed."

Mune grumbled, but she got up.

"I need you to come with me," Sanda told her.

"But where are we going?" Mune asked.

"I need you to accompany me to the local teeth carver before it is too late," Sanda whispered. "I can't let this day go by. It is my last chance to get my teeth carved."

"Really?! Do you think she will do it for you?" Mune asked.

"I have to try! This is the only day I have," Sanda said. "If I don't try, I will never know… I will just never know." She took out the dress her grandmother had made and folded it carefully under her arm.

"It is a good idea to try. I hope she will agree to carve your teeth," Mune said.

"I hope so too," Sanda replied. "Come, we need to hurry!"

They tiptoed out of the house. As they walked to the home of the local teeth carver, Sanda told her cousin all about the dream. This carver was not well known, for the people from their village preferred Buzina, but she knew how to do it. A short while later, the two girls stopped at a tiny home.

"Hodi! Hodi!" Sanda said as she knocked on the door.

"Karibu!—Welcome!" the local teeth carver replied as she opened the door. "How may I help you?"

"Please, I need to get my teeth done," said Sanda. "You are the only one who can help me."

"Sanda, you know I am not the best. No one would want me to do their teeth—" she said.

But Sanda interrupted her. "I know you can do it! All the girls my age got their teeth done yesterday, but my aunt didn't want me to go, and it is too late now because Buzina already left our village," Sanda said.

"But I am not that good!" the woman protested.

"I believe you can do it," Sanda said. "Tafadhali nisaidie—Please help me."

The carver reluctantly started working on Sanda's teeth. Sanda sat down on a stool and closed her eyes, and the carver squatted in front of her with her tools. The woman carved carefully to give Sanda's four upper front teeth a nice curved and slightly pointed shape. As her parents had said, it hurt, but it only took about twenty minutes.

Fffffffff ... The carver blew the filed tooth dust out of Sanda's mouth.

"Okay, kenua meno—Show me your teeth," the carver told Sanda. She examined them carefully.

"Safi kabisa—Perfect!" the carver said with satisfaction. "Look at yourself in the mirror, Sanda."

"Before I look, can I put on my special dress?" Sanda asked. The carver nodded, and Sanda unfolded her dress and put it on. When she twirled, the beads bounced and made a pretty jingling sound. Then Sanda approached the mirror. Oh, she felt so beautiful! Her teeth were perfectly done, and her dress was amazing. Sanda smiled at herself.

At that moment something magical happened.

The room filled with a light brighter than any she had ever seen. Everything sparkled. Sanda looked around, a little scared, but Mune and the carver cheered.

"Hooray!" cried Mune. "This is wonderful!" She stared at Sanda with disbelief, and she then rushed over to give her cousin a big hug.

The teeth carver said, "You are a special girl with a magical smile. Sanda, you have a gift: go and share it with people!"

Mune added, "You truly are special! I am so happy that you are my cousin and my best friend!"

"Ahsante sana! You are the best—Mchonga meno," said Sanda to the carver with gratitude. Bursting with joy, she and Mune headed home.

When they arrived, Aunt Nandele was very angry. She had discovered that Sanda was not home and the dress was missing. Nandele screamed louder than ever before at Sanda, and at Mune too. Sanda saw her wickedness and vowed never again to smile in her aunt's presence. Nandele did not deserve to see Sanda's magical smile.

After that day, every time Sanda smiled the space around her grew bright and the air seemed to sparkle. When people saw her smile, anyone who was sick felt better and anyone who was sad felt happy again. The whole village was filled with joy. People flocked from all around the world to witness Sanda's magical smile.

Nandele saw this and demanded that Sanda smile for her, but her niece refused.

One morning, Nandele tired of waiting for Sanda to show her smile. She grabbed Sanda and started beating her, to force her to smile for her. Sanda wept and sang, sadly, "Kelu keku wantelelaki tele Sanda yagabhaki, enseko ya Sanda toligibhona," meaning "Why are you doing this to me? You will never see Sanda's smile." Finally, Nandele gave up and sent Sanda away. But still Nandele was jealous. Everywhere Sanda went, strangers asked, "Can you smile for us please?" Sanda would smile, and amazing things happened.

"Tunakupenda, Sanda!" a group of villagers shouted when they saw Sanda passing by.

"Thank you, I love you too!" replied Sanda.

Aunt Nandele was not happy with the attention Sanda was getting. Unable to witness her niece's magical smile, she felt depressed and soon got sick. Eventually, Nandele couldn't even talk.

Sanda didn't know what to do. She was still angry about how badly her aunt had treated her. But Mune was very worried about her mother, and Sanda didn't want her best friend to be sad.

Finally, Sanda called the whole village to come together for a meeting. The village elder beat a loud rhythm on a drum to call everyone to the gathering place.

"What is it?" people asked as they gathered.

"Sanda is calling a meeting," someone answered.

"I guess we need to be there to find out what all this is about!" an old man said, heading to the gathering place.

Soon the whole village was there, young and old, men and women, everyone waiting anxiously to hear what was going on. Nandele was too weak to walk, but Sanda had asked their neighbors to bring her to the meeting. Sanda stood up before her whole village.

"I have something to share with you," she said. "You know that after my parents died, my aunt Nandele took me into her home. You know that her daughter Mune is my best friend. But you do not know that, in secret, my aunt is very cruel to me."

"Is that true?" asked Mzee Sulusi, looking Aunt Nandele in the eye. Sanda's aunt nodded slowly, for she was ashamed. "It is true," she whispered, "and I am sorry. Nisamehe, Sanda!—Forgive me!"

Sanda let out a deep sigh and cried, and then she said, "Nimekusamehe Shangazi!—I forgive you, Aunt!" And at that moment Sanda smiled wide and laughed with joy, for her heavy anger had vanished.

Suddenly, the bright light shined everywhere. The whole area sparkled, and the villagers cheered with joy! Nandele felt strong and well again, and she jumped up and ran to embrace Sanda. Tears fell from her eyes as she asked forgiveness again for all the bad things she had done. Sanda took her aunt's hand and said, "Yes, I forgive you."

Everyone quieted down as Sanda explained, "Sometimes in life, we all have to go through tough situations. At those times, we just need to be hopeful and strong, and lean on the people who truly love us. We need to forgive, too, even though it is hard, for forgiveness sets us free."

People couldn't believe what they had heard and witnessed, but Sanda's smile brought many more miracles to the village. Sanda lived a long life on Ukerewe Island, and she always shared her magical smile with any who asked. She was famous across the island, and word of her goodness spread to the whole country. Even many years after she passed away, people still talk about the *Girl with the Magical Smile.*

This book couldn't have come to life
for today's readers without
my wonderful late father,

Faustin Massinde Mugassa

(February 15th 1930 - December 7th 1999)

Author's Note

Sanda: The Girl with the Magical Smile was inspired by one of many
stories my father took time to share with me and my siblings as we grew
up in Dar-Es-Salaam, Tanzania, in the 1980s. Many years later, the story
still speaks to me. I am honored to share my own take with modern readers
without changing the story's heart: Sanda's magical smile.

While my father told this story in my first language, Kiswahili, he may have
translated the story from his mother tongue of Kikerewe, as that was the
main language used when he was born and raised on Ukerewe Island.
Today I present the story in standard American English, with some
Kiswahili dialogue included. I also wanted my readers to get an additional
part of the original story: part of a song Sanda sings in the Kikerewe language.

This story is a work of fiction, but it includes real traditions that were still
practiced in the Lake Victoria region in the early 1900s. As of the 1960s,
they had faded from popularity, but they live on in, among other places, the
book you hold in your hands.

Teeth Carving

Tooth carving is the act of using a sharp cutting tool (a knife or a chisel) to chip away some of the tooth material, to carve it into a desired shape.

- This type of tooth modification has been practiced by a variety of world cultures, mostly in Asian and African countries.
- It can also be referred to as tooth filing or tooth sharpening, depending on the culture.

Tooth carving in Tanzania

- In Tanzania, tooth carving is known as tooth sharpening. It was traditionally performed by tribes in the Lake Victoria area for around 19 centuries.
- The Zanaki tribe was one of the tribes that continued to practice the tradition until very recently.
- In its heyday in Tanzania, tooth sharpening was considered a vanity, meant to enhance or create a beautiful smile, but was also a sign of maturity in whoever went through the process.
    - o The process was painful, performed manually by elders of the community.
    - o Sharp knives and other tools were used to carve the teeth.
    - o The process was applied to the upper front teeth (maxillary central and lateral incisor).
    - o It was sign of coming of age for both girls and boys age 12 and older.
    - o The tradition was optional, but undergoing it brought great respect as a show of strength and bravery.
- The tradition is rarely practiced in the modern day; it became uncommon in the 1960s.

Tooth carving in the modern day

- In the world of modern dentistry, many procedures modify teeth by need or choice, whether to enhance beauty or to preserve healthy teeth. These processes are also painful, but with proper tools and pain-relieving measures such as anesthetics and pain medications they are easier to endure.

"Mwalimu" Julius K. Nyerere
(April 22, 1933–October 14, 1999)

Julius Kambarage Nyerere, affectionately referred to by Tanzanians as "Mwalimu" (Swahili for teacher), was the first president of the United Republic of Tanzania. He was born in the lake-shore village of Butiama, in what was then the British colony of Tanganyika. Eventually, he would lead the country to its Dec 9, 1961 independence with no bloodshed, and use Kiswahili language to unite the country's 120 dialects.

Nyerere was recognized by his beautiful smile and sharp, carved upper front teeth; his informal nickname "Mchonga" means "the one who carved his teeth." He embraced the tradition and went through the process when he was a young boy.

My special thanks to the Nyerere family, especially Julius Nyerere's son Madaraka and nephew Kambarage, for their willingness to confirm and share this information about Nyerere's experience to show readers how this tradition was embraced by many.

Glossary

Ahsante—Thank you

Ahsante sana—Thank you so much

Amka—Wake up

Hodi—May I come in?; can also be accompanied by a knocking on the door

Karibu—Welcome

Kenua meno—Show me your teeth

Kuku—Chicken

Kwaheri—Goodbye

Marahaba—Greeting of an elder to a younger person

Mchonga Meno—Teeth Carver

Meno—Teeth

Meno yangu—My teeth

Moja, mbili, tatu, nne, tano—One, two, three, four, five

Mzee—Old man or elder (term of respect)

Nakuja—I am coming

Nakupenda—I love you

Nimekusamehe—I forgive you

Nisamehe—Forgive me

Nisaidie—Help me

Njoo—Come

Nyavu—Fishnets

Nzuri—Beautiful

Safi kabisa—Very cool, perfect!

Samahani—I am sorry

Sawa—Okay

Shangazi—aunt on father's side

Shikamoo—Greeting of a younger person to an elder

Sijambo—I am doing okay

Subiri kidogo—Wait a minute

Tafadhali—Please

Toka—Go, get out

Tunakupenda—We love you

Usihofu—Do not worry

Usiku mwema—Good night

Wewe ni mtoto mzuri—You are a good kid

Sabina Mugassa Bingman, who also goes by "Sabby," was born and raised in Dar-Es-Salaam, Tanzania, the tenth of eleven children. From a very young age, she enjoyed spending time with and telling stories to her nephews and nieces. She moved to the US in 1999 and graduated from Metropolitan State University in St. Paul with a master's degree in Management Information Technology. She currently works as a Microsoft Windows server administrator.

Sabina enjoys serving in toddlers' and babies' classes at her local church. Her hobbies include running, listening to music, reading, writing, watching movies, and cooking. She and her husband Christopher are proud parents of two wonderful children, seven-year-old daughter Malaika and five-year-old son Kai. They reside in Coon Rapids, Minnesota.

authorSabina.com

Ntuli A. Aswile is a freelance artist/graphic designer whose passion for art began at a very young age. He started by drawing Pokémon cards and Power Rangers, before he was challenged by friends to create his own character—this began his journey to working as a manga/comic book artist and making his own stories. At age 15, he also started drawing portraits of real people, and has been doing so ever since. Ntuli graduated from Taylor's University in Malaysia with a degree in mass communication and media management; he currently lives in Dar-Es-Salaam, Tanzania. Hobbies include reading, traveling, making music, rapping, boxing, and messing around with Photoshop.

Follow Royal Artz By Ntuli Aswile on Instagram
@royal.artz_